For Phoebe,

In this story...

SUGAR - Hannah's toy fairy. Her skin changes colour, her magic dust can make you grow (or shrink) and she sings ALL THE TIME!

BLAZE - My toy dragon. He snorts fire and he can fly, but he is a bit scared of pretty much everything.

HANNAH - I've tried to draw her name to show you what she's like. She jumps into things and has lots of feelings and stuff.

JO - That's me! I'm just me really. But every time we have a magical adventure with Sugar and Blaze, I'm the one who writes it down.

THIS is our latest adventure...

The Sugar and Blaze Adventures
Have you read them all?

That's Rubbish! ☐

Tinselpants! ☐

Prince Charm-Bin! ☐

Nuts! ☐

THAT'S

RUBBISH!

Jenny York

ILLUSTRATED BY LUKE AND JOSIE COLLINS

For the next generation:
Josie, Hannah, Josh, Emily, Toby, Ezra,
Rebel and Niamh

with love x

Find out more about
Jenny York by
visiting
www.jennyyork.com

First published in Great Britain in 2020 by Saltaire Books, Bradford,
England.

CHAPTER ONE

It was the school holidays and my family were going camping... in a forest! Just me, my Mum and Dad and my little sister Hannah.

"Are we nearly there yet?" asked Hannah.

"You've asked that a hundred times," sighed Mum.

Dad gripped the steering wheel a little bit harder.

"You're right, Mum," I grinned, holding up my notebook to show a tally. "Hannah's asked exactly 100 times!"

//// //// ← steam from ears

//// //// ← eyes roll toward car roof.
         crazed expression.

//// //// ← This is starting to drive me insane.

//// //// ← tongue very hot

//// //// ← half way there... sparks fly out.
         opens mouth.

//// //// ← hair is on fire

//// //// ← rapid glow of lava from nose

//// //// ← 3...2...1...

//// //// ← Ka boom!

"Yes! I did it!" cried Hannah, turning to me. "You said I'd never be able to ask 100 times without Dad's head exploding!"

"Well, I've got bad news for you," grumbled Dad. "My head **has** exploded, at least twenty times since we left home."

"It has not!" said Hannah.

"Oh yes, it has!" Dad nodded. "It just grew back REALLY QUICKLY. You probably didn't notice."

Hannah and I grinned at each other.

"Thank Goodness!" said Mum, leaning forward and pointing to a sign. **"There's the campsite."**

Finally!

Dad turned down a bumpy track and in the distance was a huge field with woods around the edge. I could see kids playing and adults relaxing near tents.

The campsite was a 'no cars zone' which turned out to be a lot of work. You had to load your stuff into carts. Then you had to drag it all down this steep path to the field.

It was a long way!

We were pulling our carts down the hill when Dad whizzed past.

He'd decided to ride his!

"This is wheel-y, wheel-y good," Dad screamed. "Get it?"

"Get out!" yelled Mum. "You'll…"

Dad's cart **smashed** into a bush.

"I'm OK!" he shouted, as we ran to help. "It's

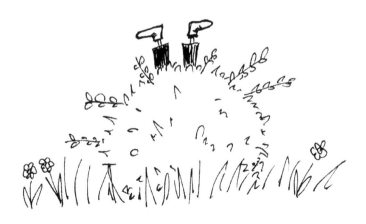

fine."

When we got to him, Dad looked a bit **embarrassed**.

"You **need** to **behave**," Mum grumbled. "No more runaway carts."

Dad pointed behind us.

"Like those ones?" he asked innocently.

Now our carts were rolling away!

"After them!" yelled Mum.

Luckily we caught them and by the time we got to the field we were all pulling our carts sensibly, like a normal family.

We found a space, right by the trees, for our big, blue tent and Mum set off back to the car to get the rest of our things. (She was muttering something about how Dad couldn't be trusted.)

That left me, Dad, and Hannah putting up the tent.

"Look at my beautiful, blue dress," he said, swishing the tent around in front of him. "I'm a princess!"

"You're not a princess, Dad," giggled Hannah.

"Aha! Maybe I'm a **KNIGHT** then," said Dad, sorting the poles into piles.

"You're really not," I grinned. "You're just a normal Dad who needs to help put up this tent before Mum gets back."

"A normal Dad!" he cried. **"What an insult!"**

He sprang to his feet, wafting one of the poles.

I am **SIR WHACK-YOUR-BUM** and I challenge you to a duel. **EN-GUARD!**

I have to admit, we did have a **teeny, tiny sword fight** with the poles at that point. Not my fault. I mean, **who turns down a sword fight**?

But eventually it was done, just as Mum arrived with the rest of the things.

"Brilliant!" said Mum.

Dad took a bow (even though Hannah and I had done most of the work), while we headed into the tent to check it out.

It <u>was</u> brilliant!

Inside there were two rooms, one for Mum and Dad, and one for us. Everything looked slightly blue, as if we were UNDERWATER. We smoothed out our sleeping bags and tucked our favourite toys inside.

Hannah had brought her toy fairy, Sugar, and I had brought my toy dragon, Blaze.

No one else knew, but Blaze and Sugar were not your average toys...

...they came to life!

Mum had started dropping hints that I was getting a bit old for a bedtime toy but I ignored her. Blaze is a **fire breathing, flying dragon** that can grow big enough to carry us.

That's the kind of toy I plan on keeping around.

Because **WEIRD STUFF** sometimes happens to Hannah and me. I probably should have mentioned that earlier.

"Kids!" called Mum, from outside. "Time to make a fire."

CHAPTER TWO

We had a barbecue for tea with **sausages** and **burgers** and lots of **ketchup.**

For dessert, Mum showed us how to toast **marshmallows** on the fire and squash them between **chocolate biscuits**.

Delicious!

After we'd all tried one, Mum started to tidy up. But Dad waved his hands at Mum, in a panic.

"Wait! I haven't had one yet," he said, spluttering **biscuit crumbs** everywhere.

Mum raised her eyebrows.

"Then, what's that in your mouth?" she asked.

"The last bit of my sausage," he tried. **"I've been chewing it for a really, really long time."**

Hannah snorted with laughter.

"You've had one!" said Mum, smiling.

Dad put on his best 'pretending to be sad' face.

"But don't I get two?" he pleaded. "After all, I am two times as big."

"You'll be two times as fat," joked Mum. "And you're already looking a bit on the round side."

Dad patted his stomach, proudly.

"This isn't fat. Didn't I tell you?" he turned to Hannah and me. **"You're going to have a little baby brother... or sister."**

Mum rolled her eyes but Dad kept going.

"I think we should call the baby Marshmallow. Marshy for short," he winked.

Everyone was giggling now. Even Mum.

Dad leapt to his feet.

"Look, it makes sense for me to have two marshmallows. Stand up, Hannah. Show Mum that I'm twice as tall."

Hannah jumped up to help, but then FROZE, EYES WIDE.

"What's up, Hannie?" asked Mum.

Hannah was staring at the woods.

"I thought I saw something..." she whispered. "... in the woods."

"Well, this is the countryside," Mum explained. "There are lots of living things in the woods. Rabbits and foxes and..."

"...FAIRIES!" interrupted Dad.

"I was talking about **real things**," said Mum.

"Fairies are **real things**," said Dad, looking offended.

He pointed upwards.

It was dark now and the sky was full of stars. I

could see loads more than normal. I guess that was part of being in the countryside.

"Look up there," said Dad. "Fairies. Millions of 'em."

Mum pursed her lips.

"Those are stars," she said.

"Nope," insisted Dad.

"Those are definitely fairies."

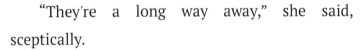

Mum peered up at the sky.

"They're a long way away," she said, sceptically.

"Good job they are!" said Dad. "Otherwise they would have heard you calling them stars. **Very rude!** They'd be coming down here to poke you with their teeny tiny wands."

Dad prodded Mum in the ribs and she laughed.

"Anyway, what were we doing?" said Dad pretending to be puzzled and scratching his head. **"Oh, I remember! We were all going to have another marshmallow."**

"Nice try," said Mum, "but I think it's time to get the kids to bed."

Dad shrugged at us.

"Ah, well," he said. **"Worth a try."**

Hannah and I rushed to put on our pyjamas. We wanted to get to bed so we could talk to Sugar and Blaze.

After hugs and "Good-nights", Mum and Dad went back outside to chat by the fire. And as soon as they were gone…

RUSTLE RUSTLE

"Is that you, Blaze?" I whispered.

"Yes," he whispered back.

"If you go down to the woods todaaaaaaaay…" sang a shrill voice.

"Hi, Sugar!" whispered Hannah.

"Shush, Sugar," hissed Blaze.

"No singing! Mum and Dad will hear."

Sugar loves singing. She sings all the time. It drives Blaze mad.

Sugar's skin glowed a cheeky purple colour in the darkness.

Because when Sugar comes to life, she changes colour a lot, depending on her feelings: red when she's angry, blue when she's sad. You get the general idea.

"So, this is camping," whispered Blaze, ignoring Sugar. "Tell us **everything.**"

Blaze loves to hear about the exciting things we do each day. He's always impressed because he finds most things a bit scary. He doesn't even like the dark.

That's probably why, after a quick zip around

the tent to stretch his wings, he came back to snuggle under my arm.

"It's been great so far," Hannah whispered.

We told them about the carts and the sword fight and the marshmallows. Thinking about it, it had been a busy day.

After a while, Hannah's voice drifted off and I heard her snuffly snores. And then, Sugar's little snore-y squeaks.

"Time to go to sleep," I told Blaze, but he didn't answer.

He must have already nodded off.

I wriggled down deeper into my sleeping bag to get cosy.

Then, I heard a noise, just outside the tent.

CRUMPLE SCRATCH

It wasn't Mum or Dad. They were still sitting by the fire. I could hear them chatting.

I lay still, listening.

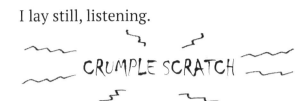

There it was again.

It sounded like an **animal** near the rubbish bag that we'd tied to the side of the tent.

"Just take it," hissed a voice.

Take what? I wondered.

But I did relax a bit. The voices meant that it wasn't some **giant, wild animal.** It was a person.

Maybe the farmer collected the rubbish each night. Maybe that's what happened on campsites.

But why hadn't he said hello to Mum and Dad? Why all the sneaking around?

I listened hard but I couldn't hear anything any more. Just Mum and Dad chatting.

VERY, VERY STRANGE!

I tried to keep listening but, eventually, I drifted off to sleep.

CHAPTER THREE

"The bin bag has disappeared," said Mum the next morning as we cleared up our breakfast things.

"I think maybe the farmer took it last night," I said, remembering the noises.

Mum frowned.

"Took our bin bag?" she said. "That's a bit odd."

"Maybe he wants a good review," Dad shrugged. "C'mon kids. Let's get going."

Mum wanted to read her book but we were heading into the woods with Dad.

We hadn't gone far into the trees before Dad

stopped dead.

"Hold on," he whispered. "We need to be careful."

"Why?" I asked, glancing around the woods. "What is it?"

"That tree," said Dad, pointing to a fat old oak. "Whatever you do, **don't touch the bark.**"

"Why?" whispered Hannah.

"Because," he hissed creeping towards it, "unless I'm mistaken, this is ...a..."

He paused, dramatically.

"... tickle tree!" he cried.

He wiggled his fingers at Hannah and she shrieked, **RUNNING AWAY**.

Dad turned to tickle me, but I was too quick. I caught up with Hannah and we **DASHED AWAY** down the path.

"Here!" I gasped eventually, pulling Hannah down with me between some rocks.

It was a great hiding place. When Dad came down the path, we would be able to spring out and make him jump. I peeked over the rocks to see if he was coming.

That's when I realised...

...WE WEREn't alonE.

"Hannah look!" I whispered, pointing down towards a nearby stream.

I couldn't believe my eyes. It was the farmer who owned the campsite.

We'd seen him walking round the field with his wife that morning, saying hello to people.

Now he was holding a big black bag.

Every so often, he would pull litter from the bag and chuck it into the water!

"That's our bin bag!" hissed Hannah, pointing. "Look! That's the packet from our marshmallows."

She was right.

"Marvellous!" said the farmer, holding up the

marshmallow packet with delight. "Just what I've been looking for. **This will make a lovely pair of pants."**

Pants? It was just a plastic bag!

The farmer tried to push one of his legs into the bag.

"These **pants** are broken!" he grumbled.

With one extra big **shove**, he lost his balance and fell into the stream.

Hannah screamed.

And a hand grabbed my shoulder...

CHAPTER FOUR

"ARGHGHHHHH!"

"Hey, hey hey! Calm down! It's only me," yelled Dad. "What on earth's the matter with you?"

"It's just...we..." I spluttered, trying to explain.

Hannah pointed down at the stream.

As Dad turned to look, the farmer struggled back to his feet. When he saw us, he tried to hide the bin bag behind his back but lost his balance again and...

"Crikey!" yelled Dad. "He needs help!!"

He ran to the bank and grabbed the farmer's hand to help him. Unfortunately, the bank was slippery.

Now, Dad was in the stream too.

"Dad!" shrieked Hannah.

"It's okay! I'm okay!" yelled Dad.

With a lot of thrashing about, Dad and the farmer both scrambled to the bank, wiping muddy hands on wet clothes.

"Bit shallow for swimming, isn't it?" said Dad, grinning.

The farmer didn't smile back.

"I was trying to clear all this litter," he said,

grumpily.

"There **is** a lot around here," agreed Dad, looking around.

"Yes. It's a shame," nodded the farmer, frowning. "So much plastic these days."

Hannah gave me a look as if to say, "What! Can you believe this guy?"

We had both seen him dumping all that litter himself.

What was he up to?

"We'd better get back to the campsite," said Dad. "Don't know about you, but I need a nice warm shower."

"Stop by the farm house on your way back and collect some fresh eggs," said the Farmer. "Free of charge. It's the least I can do."

"Aren't you coming back to the farm with us?" asked Dad.

The farmer looked Shifty but Dad didn't seem to notice.

"Not quite yet... I'm just going to finish up

here," he said.

"Take care then" said Dad, with a wink. **"No more swimming."**

The farmer nodded, snatching up his plastic bin bag, With a strange glint in his eye.

"Dad," said Hannah, as we made our way back to the farm. "That Farmer seems a bit odd."

Dad frowned.

"Why do you say that?" he asked.

"Well, Jo and I were watching him..." she began.

"...and he wasn't collecting that litter," I finished. "He was tipping it out."

Dad's eyebrows shot up in surprise.

"Really?" he asked.

"Really," said Hannah, firmly.

Dad shrugged.

"He seemed nice enough to me."

"But Dad..." I tried.

"Let's go get those free eggs, shall we?" said Dad. "Ooh! Maybe they'll let us collect them ourselves. **I've always wanted to tickle an egg out of a goat.**"

"Eggs are from hens, Dad," said Hannah, giggling. "If you tickle a goat you'll get milk."

Seriously, don't even **think** about it.

'I think what you'll *actually* get is spiked on its horns," I said, sternly.

"Nonsense," grinned Dad. "Everyone **loves** a good tickle. Look! I'll show you."

He started wiggling his fingers at us again.

We ran ahead, keeping just out of reach. But we didn't run away too far. Not after last time.

When we got back to the field, we headed for

the farmhouse. Dad knocked on the door a few times but there was no answer.

"Never mind," shrugged Dad. "We'll come back later."

Dad and Hannah walked off, arguing about milking chickens. But one of the farmhouse windows was open and something made me glance in.

The Farmer's wife was **right there,** humming cheerfully and arranging flowers in a large vase. Except, when I looked closer, **it wasn't flowers.** It was just packets and straws.

More litter!

"It still needs something," muttered the farmer's wife, stroking her chin. "Perhaps..."

She reached down to the floor.

The whole room was knee deep in litter!

Time to talk to Sugar and Blaze.

CHAPTER FIVE

"This is very, very bad!" whispered Blaze in the darkness.

As soon as we had finished tea, Hannah and I had started fake-yawning. Mum had looked surprised, but Dad said the fresh air was working miracles and packed us off to bed.

We'd just finished telling the toys about the

strange things that had happened that day.

"It definitely sounds like magic...magic...ma-ma-ma..." sang Sugar.

"Yes, magic! No need to sing!" worried Blaze, looking towards the door.

"So what do we do?" I asked.

The tent went quiet as we all tried to figure it out.

Then, just outside the tent...

RUSTLE RUSTLE RUSTLE

"The rubbish bag," hissed Hannah. "That crazy farmer is stealing it again."

"Shhh," I whispered.

RUSTLE RUSTLE RUSTLE

"Are you **sure** about this?" said a rough voice.

"We **have** to. We have no choice," growled another voice.

RUSTLE RUSTLE RUSTLE

"**This is ridiiiiiiiculous**," Sugar half-sang, half-whispered. **"I'm going out there to kick his packet-panted bum bum!"**

"No, you can't," squeaked Blaze. "It could be **dangerous.**"

But the sparkle of Sugar's wings had already whizzed over to the zipped up door on the side of the tent.

"Come on," I whispered, scrambling out of my sleeping bag. "We have to know what's happening."

I unzipped the door as quietly as I could, so we could peek at the farmer. But it wasn't him!

Two foxes were tugging bin bags away in their teeth. It was slow going but they were almost to the edge of the wood.

"The cheeky little things!" exclaimed Sugar and set off after them.

"Sugar, wait," whispered Hannah, pulling on her boots and DARTING after her.

The foxes had seen them coming! One was

frozen in panic. The other was trying to pull a rubbish bag on its own and not getting very far.

Don't move.
Pretend to be a tree.
An **invisible** tree.

"We can't let them go running off alone," I whispered to Blaze, pulling on my boots. "Come on!"

As we left the tent, more f°Xe∫ sprang out from the w°°d. Working together, they lifted the bags and sped away.

We caught up with Sugar and Hannah, and we CHASED the f°Xe∫ into the w°°d. I could see the outline of Hannah's body ahead of me, **but only just**. Blaze was panting somewhere above my head.

We **RAN AND RAN** until we burst into a clearing by the stream.

But the **foxes**...

...were gone.

In the moonlight, a weeping willow tree trailed its branches into the water.

But that wasn't the main thing to see.

Next to the stream, rippling in the night breeze, was a

mountain

of

litter.

Blaze whimpered.

I tiptoed forwards, **tiny pine cones** crunching under my boots.

Sugar peered up at the **tower of rubbish**, tall as a house.

"what is this?" breathed Hannah.

A sudden gust of wind made the pile shudder and I shuddered too.

Because we were in the **woods**...in the **dark.**

ALONE!

Then a **strange** clacking noise **echoed** around the clearing, like **something** was laughing at us.

ck-ck-ck-ck-ck-ck-ck

ck-ck-ck-ck-ck-ck-ck

ck-ck-ck-ck-ck-ck-ck

NOT ALONE.

CHAPTER SIX

"That's rubbish," squeaked a tiny voice.

"Who's there?" called Hannah.

"Are you....lost?" asked a chilling voice from the darkness.

"No," lied Blaze, but his voice wobbled with fear.

There was a noise in the branches above. Hannah pulled me until we were **back to back, ready to fight.**

For a split second, I saw a flash of white in the dark and my mind gasped the word 'ghost'.

But as it spiralled down and landed at our

feet, I could see it was nothing more dangerous...

than a **magpie**.

"Hello there,"
said the Magpie.
"I'm Magnus!
Sorry if we scared you."

"We?" questioned Blaze.

Magnus began to preen his feathers and out

fell a **caterpillar**.

"**That's rubbish,**" squeaked the caterpillar, as it hit the pine cones.

"**Who are you?**" demanded Hannah.

"Us?" asked the magpie. "Why, we are the guardians of the forest."

"**That's rubbish,**" squeaked the caterpillar.

"**Guaaaaaaaaaardians**? **Well, you aren't doing a very good job,**" sang Sugar, pointing at the litter pile. "**That's...**"

"**...Rubbish!**" interrupted the caterpillar.

"**Ex- aaaaaaaa- ctly!**" sang Sugar.

Magnus looked like he was frowning in confusion but it's hard to tell with a magpie, especially in the dark.

"Why is your friend singing?" he asked Blaze.

"Why does **your** friend only say the word 'rubbish'?" snapped Blaze, defensively.

"Touché!" said Magnus.

"Same to you!" snarled Blaze.

I'd never seen Blaze defend Sugar before. It was very cute but this was getting us nowhere fast.

Hannah was obviously thinking the same thing because she stepped forward.

"Is that really all your caterpillar says?" she asked.

"Yes. I'm afraid so," said Magnus.

"Over and over?"

"Yes."

"Well, that really is..." Hannah searched for the right word, "...rubbish!"

"Rubbish!" agreed the caterpillar.

He nodded at Hannah happily, clearly

thinking he'd found a friend.

Magnus gave a deep sigh and scooped him up in his beak. I was pretty sure the little guy was a going to be a magpie snack but Magnus just shoved him back in his feathers.

"The caterpillar gets over-excited," he explained. "You see, he loves **rubbish**. We're both **crazy** about recycling."

"You recycle rubbish?" asked Hannah.

"Yes!"

"So *you* sent those foxes to steal our bin," I guessed.

"**No, no, no!**" said Magnus, horrified. "We collect litter that is polluting the wood. We don't **steal** it."

"That's rubbish," squeaked the caterpillar, sticking out its head.

Magnus glared at him and the caterpillar ducked back into the feathers.

"Why?" I asked.

"To keep the forest clean, of course," he said proudly. "Magpies like collecting things, so we're the obvious animals for the job."

"And the caterpillar?" asked Hannah.

Magnus shrugged...I think. **Again, it's hard to be sure with a magpie.**

"Just a friend to chat to," he said. "Now, I should take you back to your campsite. The forest can be **DANGEROUS**."

"That's rubb..." the caterpillar stopped and then nodded.

I guess he agreed about the dangerous bit. I was starting to agree too.

"Let's get going, then," I suggested.

Magnus began to lead us out of the clearing.

It was a good job he wanted to take us home because I'd have guessed the campsite was in the opposite direction.

"Have you...er... met any of the other woodland folk," Magnus asked as we walked.

"No, we haven't. Waiiiiiiiiiit a minute! Do you have fairies here?" asked Sugar. **"Boy fairies?"**

"Sugar!" gasped Blaze.

"What?" sniffed Sugar. "I'm not getting any younger, you know."

"You're a toy," grumbled Blaze. "You're not getting any younger or any older."

Sugar grinned in the moonlight.

"Still, it's niiiiiiiiiice to make new frieeeeeeends!"

"Shhhh! Yes!" snapped Magnus, glancing around nervously. "There are fairies. Lots of fairies. Now, if you could just be a bit more quiet..."

This guy really didn't get Sugar at all. Sugar hates being quiet!

"Fabuuuuuuuuuulous!" sang Sugar. **"You know, I think I remember a song about a magpie..."**

One for sorrow. Two for joy. Three for a girl and four for a boy. A boy boy b-b-boy. A beautiful fairy boy just for meeeeeeee!

Hannah giggled.

"That's **not** how that song goes," grumbled Blaze. "You're making that last bit up."

Sugar turned a happy yellow colour and stuck her tongue out at him.

Magnus was moving more quickly now. The white feathers made him easy to see in the dark.

But he was still hard to **follow** because we weren't on any kind of path. Branches whacked us and nettles swooshed around our boots, stealthy stingers in the darkness.

"Are you **sure** this is the right way," I asked.

"Oh, yes! I..." Magnus stopped suddenly. "Shhh!"

We all froze but somewhere close by a twig

snapped.

"Campsite's that way," blurted Magnus, wafting his wing back the way we just came. "You'll be safe now. Bye!"

"That's rubbiiiiiiiiish," squeaked the caterpillar, his voice fading, as Magnus swooped away.

Again, I agreed with the caterpillar. There was **no way** we were safe.

Then, I saw them.

Yellow eyes...

...sharp teeth, gleaming

in the darkness.

Blaze gave a whimper.

I felt Hannah slip her hand into mine and squeeze. It was our **secret signal**. It meant *get ready*.

CHAPTER SEVEN

We were surrounded by foxes.

Some **GROWLED**, low in their throats. Others were silent. The silent ones were by far the worst because they looked tensed, **READY TO POUNCE**.

I glanced at Hannah and realised she was holding a branch looking dangerous.

How?!

That girl is like a ninja sometimes. Not that I'm complaining. Hannah looked ready to defend us all. Although, maybe we could work this out without starting a fight... Maybe?

"You!" shrieked Sugar, pointing at the biggest fox. **"You stole our biiiiiiiiin, you rotten old bag of fleeeeeeeeeeeeas."**

Maybe not!

"Sugar!" wailed Blaze, somehow making her name sound a lot like **'stop talking!'**

But the growling had stopped. Instead, I heard an unexpected sound.

Huh huh huh huh!

Deep, growl-like chuckling.

The foxes were laughing.

"I sure did, sweet thing," said the biggest fox, giving Sugar a wink. "And I may have a flea or two, but less of the 'old'. That's just **mean!**"

"Well..." said Sugar. **"I mean...ermm..."**

Sugar was speechless. Song-less. Everything-less. That had to be a first.

"A – hem!" said a tinkling voice.

I'd been so busy looking at all those **sharp,**

foxy teeth that I'd missed the most surprising thing.

Riding on the back of each **fox**...

...was a fairy.

Each one was the size of a human hand with a pair of delicate, sparkling wings. And they were every colour of the rainbow.

"Dad was right!" I murmured.

The fairy on the largest fox smiled at me. Most of the fairies wore **beech**

nut shells like helmets but this fairy wore a band of **silver birch bark,** like a crown.

"I am Princess Snowtip," she said. "And

we are the fox fairies,"

"Fox fairies?" sang Sugar.

"Yes. We Woodland fairies name our tribes after the animals we ride," she explained.

"Then I wouldn't want to be a hedgehog fairy," muttered Sugar, under her breath. **"All those spikes up your bum!"**

"What's that, dear?" asked the princess.

"Oh, nothing at aaaaaaaall," sang Sugar, smiling sweetly.

Princess Snowtip frowned, suspiciously.

"Your Highness, may I ask..." said Hannah, trying to distract her. "Why were you taking our rubbish?"

"To stop the **magpies** taking it," she said, grimly.

"**Oh, it's okay,**" sang Sugar. "**They're recyyyyyyycling it.**"

The **foxes barked angrily**.

"I'm afraid not," said Princess Snowtip, frowning. "Magpies have always liked shiny things for their nests. But a few weeks ago, something changed."

"Dark Magic filled the wood," growled her fox. "The **magpies** started to act...differently."

"Now the **humans** are changing, too," added Princess Snowtip. "They bring extra

48

litter to the woods!"

The foxes shook their heads, sadly.

"And the magpies have been collecting huge amounts of rubbish and taking it somewhere," said Princess Snowtip.

"We can't find the exact place," growled the fox. "We think the magic is hiding it."

"But we know where it is," gasped Hannah. "There's a big pile. We just came from it."

"It's in a clearing..." I said, trying to describe what I could remember. "...by the stream... near a weeping willow tree."

"The Hollow!" breathed the princess. "Of course."

"How big was it?" barked the fox.

"As tall as a house," whimpered Blaze.

"Was there..." Princess Snowtip looked

afraid to finish. "Was there anything around the pile? On the floor?"

I thought hard.

"I don't think so," I said. "Just some pine cones."

The foxes and fairies gasped.

Then the foxes went wild again, barking and howling.

YAP YAP YAP OOOOW!

Everyone was talking at once.

"No!"

"They wouldn't!"

"Surely not."

"I'm going to get that magpie and stiiiiiiiiick his caterpiiiiiiiiiiiillar..."

That last one was Sugar (she just likes to join in).

"What?" I asked. "What is it?"

"A ring of pine cones is sort of like "Step 1" in

most woodland magic," explained Princess Snowtip. "My guess is, they're waking the litter," she added. "Turning it into a **MONSTER.**"

"We'll need **help** to defeat a **MONSTER!**" cried a yellow fairy. "We must ask for a magical gift from the Queen of the Fairies."

There was lots of excited nodding from the

fairies and a few yip-yaps of fox agreement.

"There isn't time to go to the Queen," said another. "Let's go straight to The Hollow and fight the magpies."

A lot of the fairies seemed to like this idea too. Princess Snowtip looked undecided.

"What if we went to the fairy queen," offered Hannah.

"Then **you** could go straight to The Hollow," I added.

"That might work," agreed the princess, nodding thoughtfully.

"**One teeeeeeeeny problem**," sang Sugar. "**How do we fiiiiiind her?**"

A fox moved out from the group. On its back was a handsome boy fairy. He leaped from the fox, did two perfect somersaults and landed

in front of Princess Snowtip.

"**Oh my!**" sighed Sugar.

"I can show them the way," he said.

The princess nodded.

"Very well, Braveleaf," she agreed. "Take them to the Queen as fast as you can."

Braveleaf gave a low bow.

"As for the rest of us," said Princess Snowtip, "we attack, at once. **Onward!**"

She charged off, into the darkness and the other foxes galloped after her.

Once she was gone Braveleaf gave a big sigh.

"Well, I think I've dodged a bullet there," he muttered, which didn't strike me as very brave. "Let's get going, shall we?"

Sugar flew straight to his side.

"**Is it faaaaar,**" she sang, batting her eyelashes.

"Not far at all, but it'll be tricky to get to her.

The Queen of the Fairies is an owl fairy- **very smart** and they protect themselves well."

"**You seem smart**," sang Sugar, adoringly. "**I bet you'll get us there in no time at all**."

Braveleaf looked puzzled. He opened his mouth to say something, then seemed to change his mind. Instead he turned to Blaze.

"I've always wanted to be a Dragon Fairy rather than a Fox Fairy," said Braveleaf hopefully. "Can you blast fire?"

"Erm... yes," said Blaze, looking uncomfortable.

Blaze didn't like attention. Even the good kind.

"**Amazing!**" said Braveleaf. "**Much cooler than a fox!**"

Blaze blushed, sending his blue cheeks purple.

"**Excuse me...**" sang Sugar trying to get the attention back to herself.

But before she could say any more, the soil of the path under our feet began to tremble.

"Run!" shouted Braveleaf.

It felt like an EARTHQUAKE. The path started to bulge up and break apart. I stumbled and fell. Hannah yanked me to my feet and WE RAN.

Then, in a

MASSIVE EXPLOSION

the forest floor **crumbled to bits**.

The others flew up towards the stars and safety.

But without a path, Hannah and I dropped

into

THE

DEEP

DARKNESS

OF THE EARTH.

CHAPTER EIGHT

We were **FALLING, fast!**

Then **BUMPING.**

Then **SLIDING.**

DEEPER

and

DEEPER.

Finally, we **SKIDDED TO A STOP.**

The tunnel had opened out into a massive underground chamber, lit dimly with torches.

"This night just gets worse and worse," said Hannah, sitting up beside me and checking out the grazes on her arms. "How are we supposed to get back to the surface?"

"Not the main problem, Han," I whispered, pointing.

All around the chamber, tunnels led off into the dar̶k̶n̶e̶s̶s̶. Peering from each one was a mole, which might have been cute, except these moles were as big as dogs.

Blown up to dog-size, each slimy, snuffling nose looked like a pink octopus. Every paw had five claws and every claw looked as sharp as a kitchen knife.

"What do we do?" hissed Hannah.

"No idea," I whispered.

There was a wet, snotty noise as one of

the moles felt his way towards us.

Riding the mole, was a tiny something, hidden in a grey cloak.

I suspected we were about to meet our first mole fairy.

"Wandering around the forest at night," came the calm, quiet voice. "Explain yourselves."

As she removed her hood, I could see steel grey skin and hair. She wore grey gloves and her hands were clenched into fists. From the knuckles of the gloves poked long,

razor-sharp spikes.

I took a deep breath.

"We're looking for The Fairy Queen," I

said, as bravely as I could. "Is she, erm... here?"

The tunnels echoed with laughter.

"The Fairy Queen does not live in the tunnels," sneered the fairy.

"But this **is** one of the entrances," added the mole.

"Oh, *well done*, Trevor!" said the fairy sarcastically. "Maybe you should tell them about *all* the secret entrances."

"Well, there's one in the...." began the mole.

"Stop talking, you nincompoop!" snapped the fairy.

"Haha! She said poop!" sniggered another mole.

"Look," I tried. "If this is an entrance, please could you let us in, or through, or..."

"We don't let people **in,**" she interrupted, coldly. "We keep people **out.**"

She started to move towards us with a nasty glint in her eyes.

"And we take our job **very** seriously," she snarled. "**No one** gets past the mole fairies."

Next to me, Hannah took my hand and squeezed.

"Jo, look!" she breathed.

"Sort of busy, right now," I hissed back.

"Jo!"

She was staring at the other side of the cavern. There, resting on golden tracks, was a carriage. It was pale blue and decorated with golden owls.

"Is that...?" I said.

"What are you **muttering** about," snapped the mole fairy. "You're not **supposed** to mutter. You're **supposed** to shake with **FEAR**."

"Or you could beg for mercy," suggested the mole, cheerfully. "I do like a bit of begging for mercy."

"Sorry," shrugged Hannah. "We're not really the begging type..."

And instead she **RAN** straight at the mole, **yelling** and **waving her arms.**

"RARGHGHGHHHHH"

Moles can't see very well but they hear things perfectly. This one could definitely hear the crazy yelling. He squealed and started rearing up in fear.

Then, just as Hannah was about to **BARGE** into them, she **DARTED** round to the right and

NIPPED past.

I told you she was like a ninja.

Hannah had now used up all the 'element of surprise' stuff which left me with...well, not very much.

Moles and fairies rushed from the other tunnels. I did my best to **RUN** after Hannah, **DODGING** the screeching, slobbering moles and furious, grey fairies.

Hannah, was **PUSHING** at the carriage to get it started. It was heavy but it was starting to **MOVE**. I threw myself against it with all my might and it started to **ROLL** down the tracks, **PICKING UP SPEED.**

"Get in!" yelled Hannah.

We **JUMPED** into the carriage, strapping ourselves in. The carriage seemed to realise it had passengers and it **WHIZZED OFF** down the rails leaving the furious fairies shaking their fists.

WE RACED DOWNWARDS

...AND THEN UP AGAIN

...AND THEN DOWN *-aaaaahhh!* **AGAIN,**

until I thought I might be sick. The wind whipped against my face making my eyes water. "How do we control this thing?" Hannah yelled. I felt around in the darkness. The carriage was just seats and edges. **No handles. No levers No buttons**.

"I don't think we can," I yelled back.

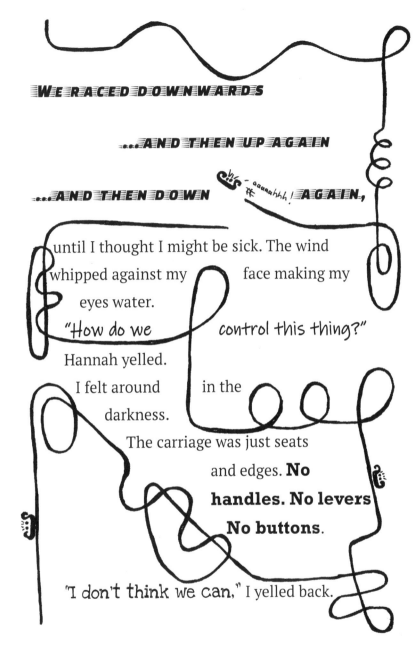

CHAPTER NINE

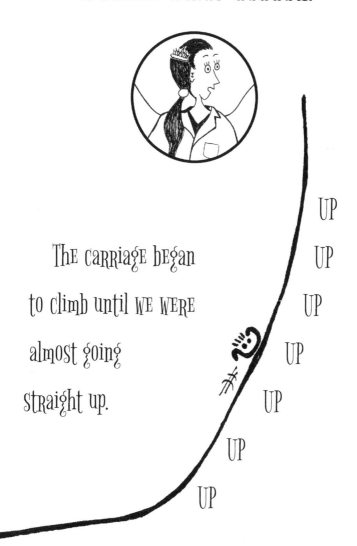

The carriage began to climb until WE WERE almost going straight up.

UP
UP
UP
UP
UP
UP
UP

It felt like the first bit of a roller-coaster. I wasn't looking forward to the **next bit** where we dropped back down again.

Luckily, before that could happen, the carriage pulled up to a bright, white platform.

"You have reached your destination.

Land of the Fairy Queen.

Thank you for travelling with Fairy Rail..." said a polite voice from beneath the seats, before adding, rather crossly, **"... well, get out then! Chop, chop!"**

The carriage tipped us out.

On the platform, there was a single wooden door with a handwritten sign.

"The carriage said Land of the Fairy Queen!" said Hannah. "This has to be it."

I pushed open the door and we walked through.

"Oh wow!" whispered Hannah. "I was expecting butterflies and flowers and stuff...like in all the fairy tales."

"This is way cooler," I said, and it really was!

We were in a white lab stretching on as far as the eye could see. Fairies were flitting around, doing experiments and making notes. Working alongside them were **hundreds of owls**.

In fact, one of those **owls** was soaring over to us **right now!**

"**You**-hoo-hoo-hooo can't be here!" it hooted angrily. "**Whoo**-whoooo-who-whooooo do you think you are?"

More **owls** were flying over with curious expressions.

"This is **new**- hoo-hoo-hoooooo," said one.

"**Who**-hoo-hoo-hoo-hooo are **you**-hoo-hoo-hoo?" asked another.

"I need a poo -hoo – hoo hooo!" said another (No idea why it wanted us to know that.)

Before we could say anything though, a fairy came flying through the crowd.

"What's going on here?" she demanded.

Her lab coat was so white it gleamed and her long black hair was pinned in place with a silver, crown-shaped hair slide. Fluttering and flapping by her side, was a grumpy looking **owl**.

"Good gracious!" gasped the fairy. "Children!"

"I really don't know why I pay those mole fairies," she sighed. "What's the point of having a secret lab if human children can just wander in?"

"**True**-hoo-hooo-hooo," agreed the **owl**.

"The moles did try to stop us," I said.

"With big knives," added Hannah.

"Knives?" gasped the fairy. "I never said they could have knives! Granger, make a note. I'll need to have a serious word. And I'm shrinking them back to normal mole size! Letting people through AND knives!"

The owl pulled an electrical device from his feathers and pecked a note.

"Well, if you don't mind, we're rather busy here..." she said, ushering us back towards the door.

"Are you scientists?" I asked.

"Well, yes," she admitted. "Fairies protect the wild places of this world. Science is how we do it, these days!"

"Lots of **polu**- hoo-hoo-hoo- **tion**," grumbled Granger, the owl. "We research **solu**-hoo-hoo-

70

hoo-**tions**."

"And we really must get on, so off you go."

She held the door open, pointing back to the railway platform.

"No, wait," I said."We need to talk to The Queen of the Fairies. We need her help!"

"Well, that would be me," she admitted. "But my dear, I don't **help** people. Goodness no, I'm a leader. I believe in **helping** people to **help** themselves."

"There were waaaaay too many helps in that sentence," said Hannah shaking her head in confusion.

The queen smiled.

"My dears, if you've spotted a problem in the forest, then I formally grant you permission to fix it!" said the Queen.

"WHAT!" cried Hannah. "So you aren't going to help us?"

"Why, my dear," she said smugly. "I just did!"

"No you didn't!" said Hannah crossly. "The

magpies have built a tower of litter and now they are going to wake it up and make a monster! And you're leaving it to us?"

"Well my dear if you don't mind my saying so, it does all sound rather dangerous..."

"That's because it is!" snapped Hannah.

"And I'm a Queen, you see, so I don't really..."

"Look," I interrupted, "if you won't come with us to help then fine! But we came here to get a gift and we're not leaving without one!"

"A gift?" said the Queen.

"Yes," I nodded. "A magical gift, to defeat the **LITTER MONSTER**. Like a Ninja Bin, or something".

"Oh..." she said, looking relieved. "OK, I

might have something like that."

The Queen slipped the crown-shaped slide from her hair and placed it into Hannah's hand.

"It will need to **touch the monster's head** to work," she said.

Hannah is normally the polite one but she was just glaring.

"OK," I nodded. Then I made myself add, "Thanks."

"Yes...well..." said the queen watching Hannah warily. "Let's send you back to where you need to be, shall we?"

"Is there any chance you could find our friends, too?" I asked.

The queen stretched out her arms, sensing the forest, frowning with concentration.

"One blue dragon, one purple fairy who is currently singing..." she pulled a face, "and a boy fox fairy?"

"Yes, that's them!" said Hannah forgetting to be mad in her excitement.

The Queen nodded. Then she closed her eyes, raised her arms and wiggled her fingers.

In the blink of an eye, we were back in the forest.

Sugar, Blaze and Braveleaf were in a tangled, confused heap next to us.

And I could hear two familiar voices arguing nearby...

CHAPTER TEN

"I'm starting to think this is a **bad idea,**" said a voice.

It was Magnus, the magpie.

"That's rubbish," squeaked his caterpillar friend.

"**You're right.** Of course you are. We're doing the right thing. The Litter Queen will rise and I will be her favourite."

"That's rubbish."

"**What!** Why don't you think I'll be her favourite? You've been listening to the other magpies, haven't you? **Admit it!**"

"That's rubbish."

The argument continued as we crept forward, hardly daring to breathe, and peeked into the clearing.

The litter pile stood just as high as ever. Dotted around it were cages made from litter and inside...

"No!" gasped Hannah.

The fairies and their foxes were all trapped. The foxes paced back and forth, snapping and snarling at the bars of the cage. But the fairies looked dazed. Some of them were crying quietly.

Magpies perched in the trees around the litter pile- hundreds of them, each tiny beak calling out.

ck-ck-ck-ck-ck

ck-ck-ck-ck-ck

ck-ck-ck-ck-ck

And more were arriving all the time. The calling was getting louder and louder.

Then the plastic pile began to rustle and move.

It started to grow a face with **MOULDY, MILK-CARTON TEETH** and **PALE, PIZZA BOX EYES**.

It was HORRIBLE!

Soon, the face started to rise up from the ground on

TWO TOWERING LEGS OF LITTER.

We needed to act fast before that thing grew a body and arms.

"How did we all end up back here?" asked Sugar, astonished.

"Never mind that now," hissed Blaze in the darkness. "Hannah, Jo, did you get a magical gift?"

I nodded.

"So what is it?" hissed Sugar.

Hannah held up the crown hair slide.

"Oh, that's **pretty!**" said Sugar reaching for it.

"Shhhhhh," hissed Blaze.

Sugar glared at Blaze and turned an angry red colour which wasn't going to help us stay hidden.

But the **MONSTER** didn't seem to have noticed us.

Not yet.

"The Fairy Queen said it has to go on the monster's head to work," I said, quietly.

"You've got to be kidding," hissed Sugar. "That thing is **taller than the trees**! And look at it's **teeth**!"

All our eyes turned back to the **MONSTER**. It had grown a body now with two stubby arms.

"SHE IS WAKING," cried Magnus, hopping around at the monster's feet. **"Our Litter Queen is waking."**

Encouraged, the magpies started to clack even louder

ck-ck-ck-ck-ck-ck-ck

ck-ck-ck-ck-ck-ck-ck

ck-ck-ck-ck-ck-ck-ck

until...

"ENOUGH!"

roared the litter monster. IT WAS ALIVE!

The **magpies** stopped. In their cages, the **foxes** and **fairies** froze. Everyone held their breath.

"**I HAVE LIFE,**" growled the monster. "**YOU,** my **MAGPIE MINIONS**, have been **FAITHFUL**. As I **DESTROY THE WOOD**, you alone will not be

CHOKED in my **PLASTIC GRIP OF DEATH.**"

The **magpies** click-clacked their thanks. Or possibly they were just clacking in terror.

Hard to say.

"BUT I STILL NEED HANDS. YOU CAN'T HAVE A PLASTIC GRIP OF DEATH WITHOUT FINGERS. GO, FETCH ME MORE LITTER!" ordered the monster. **"GO!"**

The **magpies** scattered in an instant. All except for Magnus. He **tried** to fly off but the monster pinned him to the ground with its littery leg.

"NOT YOU, YOU IDIOT," it growled. **"WE NEED TO TALK."**

"Erm, of course, My Queen," said Magnus, sounding tERRifiEd.

"QUEEN?!" roared

the monster. **"I'M NOT A QUEEN!"**

"Erm...you're not?"

"OF COURSE NOT," growled the monster.

"I'M A KING. ISN'T THAT OBVIOUS? DON'T YOU THINK I'M HANDSOME?"

"Erm..."

"I'VE GOT PACKETS, WRAPPERS," he pointed at himself, **"PIZZA BOX EYES – I'VE GOT IT ALL. CHECK OUT MY SMILE."**

The litter monster leaned down and bared its milk-carton teeth. Close up, the smell of all that

litter must have been dreadful.

I could understand why Magnus was finding it hard to think of a compliment.

"I have an idea," whispered Sugar. "Give me the slide."

"Are you sure you know what you're doing?" asked Hannah, handing it to her.

Sugar nodded.

"I may not understand **boys**," said Sugar, glaring at Braveleaf, "but I do understand **style**."

She narrowed her eyes, studying the **MONSTER**.

"Braveleaf! Blaze!" she hissed. "You can both fly, so you'll need to chase away Magnus."

"Or..." said Braveleaf, "...maybe we should, erm, not do that. We should, erm, go look for the other magpies."

"What!" frowned Sugar. **"How would that help?"**

"Well, because...because..." Braveleaf looked flustered.

Blaze put a gentle paw on his shoulder.

"I'm scared, too," said Blaze quietly. "Let's do it anyway, eh?"

Braveleaf stared at him. Finally, he nodded. Blaze grinned.

"Hop on my back, **Dragon Fairy,**" winked

Blaze. "Let's do this together!"

"Seriously?" asked Braveleaf, beaming.

Blaze nodded and Braveleaf flew up to perch between his wings.

"Ready," said Braveleaf, proudly.

I looked back to Sugar.

"What do you want us to do?" I whispered.

"You're with me!" said Sugar, turning a nervous pale blue. **"Just follow my lead."**

CHAPTER ELEVEN

We looked back to the **MONSTER**. Down in the clearing, Magnus had finally thought of something to say.

"You are very **handsome**, my King," he grovelled. "I've never seen anyone **so handsome...**"

For a moment, the litter monster looked like it might be trying to smile. But then the caterpillar popped up.

"That's rubbish," he squeaked.

"WHAAAAT!"

screamed the **MONSTER**, exploding with **RAGE**.

"**Now!**" yelled Sugar. "**Go! Go!**"

We **BURST** into the clearing. Blaze and Braveleaf roared a battle cry and **RACED** towards Magnus, shouting the most terrifying things they could think up.

"You'll never have another nap ever again!" threatened Blaze.

"I'll make you ride a hedgehog!" yelled Braveleaf. **"See how your bottom likes that!"**

Magnus *screamed* and **FLEW OFF** into the woods, and they went **HURTLING** after him.

And we walked forward to face the monster.

"HUMANS!"

snarled the Litter King. "**AND A FAIRY.** I suppose you've come to try to **DESTROY ME?** Just like all those **GROTTY LITTLE ROTTERS.**"

He pointed towards the cages of fairies.

"Oh no! Not at all," lied Sugar.

"**GOOD!**" snapped the King. "Because I'm here to stay. Plastic litter can last for hundreds of years, you know!"

"**Really? Hundreds of years? How incredible,**" gasped Sugar, faking admiration.

"**AND THAT'S NOT ALL,**" added the King, proudly. "Plastic just like this is building up all around the world. Soon, I will rule an army. **THOUSANDS,** just like me. Well, not quite as **FABULOUS or STYLISH** as me but you get the idea."

"**More of you would be lovely**," smiled Sugar, sweetly. "**You're so handsome.** And I should know. **I'm a beauty expert.**"

"**YOU ARE?**"

"She is!" I chipped in.

"She really is," agreed Hannah. "She helps me pick my clothes every day so that I look amazing."

The monster paused, considering.

"**COULD YOU...**" said the litter monster. "**COULD YOU HELP ME LOOK AMAZING....FOR WHEN I CHOKE THE EARTH AND EVERYTHING. I WANT TO LOOK MY BEST.**"

"**Of course,**" said Sugar. "It's all about **accessories.**"

In a flash, I realised Sugar's plan. **And it was brilliant.**

"**Your overall look is great,**" she said. "You've got **packets, cartons, wrappers.**"

Sugar counted things off on her fingers and the monster nodded eagerly.

"**You just need something that says 'KING',**" said Sugar, "**and I have just the thing.**"

She pulled out the crown hair slide and it sparkled in the moonlight.

"**OH, THAT IS POSH,**" growled the monster.

"WHERE DOES IT GO?"

"On the top of your head," said Hannah.

"So it won't get in your way when you're **choking and killing stuff**," I added, trying to help.

The monster nodded.

"Shall I pop it in for you?" asked Sugar.

We all held our breath, waiting.

"GO ON THEN," growled the monster. "I suppose a **BIT OF SPARKLE** won't hurt."

Sugar gave us a 'be-ready-to-run-for-it' look and flew forwards.

"WAIT!" said the monster, frowning.

Sugar paused in mid air.

"YOU GOT HERE JUST AS THAT DRAGON CHASED OFF MY MAGPIE SERVANT," said the monster, thoughtfully.

"What dragon?" asked Sugar, innocently, but her wings started to buzz a little faster.

The monster raised an arm towards the sky.

"**THAT ONE!**" he growled, pointing.

Sure enough, Blaze and Braveleaf were **SPEEDING BACK** towards us **CHASED** by a massive cloud of black and white magpies.

"**Heeeeeeeeeelp,**" yelled Blaze as he **WHIZZED** past, looping the monster and surrounding it with a flapping magpie cloud.

The time for tricks was over.

Sugar **FLEW UP** through the flurry of wings **towards the monster's head.** But the Litter King had guessed she was up to something.

"NO! RARGHGH!"

he **roared** and he swung a stubby litter arm, **knocking Sugar out of the sky.**

She landed in the dirt on the opposite side of the clearing.

"Sugar!" screamed Hannah.

We **RAN** to help but Sugar had already **jumped up** and dusted herself down.

"**I'm OK**," she said. "**Free the prisoners. Blaze needs back up.**"

The **MONSTER** was trying to swat Blaze, too. So far, he hadn't hit him but he was **knocking magpies in** every **direction** and

ROARING WITH RAGE.

"SMASH THE ROTTERS! RARGHGH!"

Sugar tried to take off but one of her wings didn't buzz. It was bent at a funny angle.

"Sugar, is it broken?" gasped Hannah.

Sugar glared at the monster, turning volcano-lava red.

"Not as broken as he's going to be," she said, grimly.

Since she couldn't fly, she SPRINTED for one of the monster's legs and started to climb.

Hannah tugged at my arm.

"We have to free the fairies and foxes," she yelled. "Come on!"

We **RAN** around the cages, **ripping them apart**. **Foxes** leaped out and began to throw themselves at the monster's legs. Fairies flew into the air and started to **battle** the magpies.

Sugar was still climbing, **clinging on for dear life,** as the monster spun round, waving his arms.

I kept ripping at the cages until Hannah tugged at my sleeve.

"Jo, look!" she yelled, pointing to the Litter King.

Sugar was sitting on top of the monster's head, riding him as he staggered around.

"Check me out!" she yelled over the noise of the battle. **"I'm a monster fairy!"**

And she clipped the crown slide onto a wisp of its crisp packet hair.

"NOOOOO!"

roared the monster.

Packets and wrappers began to drop from the monster's head like **bad dandruff**. Then, his **legs started to crumble**, first one, then the other, sending him **sprawling to the floor**.

"NOOOOO!"

he roared.

"Ck-ck-ck-ck-ck," screamed the magpies.

The **wind whipped up**, until a *gale* was blowing round the clearing. It was carrying away litter and **magpies**, gust by gust.

The last few cages fell apart. The fairies

clung to the trees. The **foxes** crouched low to the ground. The **MONSTER** was roaring furiously as he came apart, bit by bit.

Hannah and I clung together, as a

Finally, the wind died down and everything was still. I opened one eye to peek, **still a bit**

scared about what I might see.

The litter was knee deep in some places. Fairies and foxes sat half-buried in the rubbish like children in a ball pool. It was an **absolute mess – but the monster... was gone.**

In the centre of it all, stood an extremely dirty, but triumphant, Sugar.

"Looking good is about actions, not hair clips!" she announced to her dazed audience. "**And, of course, it's about**

expreeeeesiiiiiiiiiiiiiiiiiing

yourseeeeeeeeeeeeelf!"

Blaze came to land next to her. He pulled a face at the singing.

"Well-done, Noisy," he said.

She winked at him, turning a happy yellow colour.

Braveleaf sprang from Blaze's back.

His jaw was practically on the floor.

"You...you did it?" he stammered at Sugar. **"You're amazing."**

"Yes, I aaaaaaaaaaaaaaam...." she sang. "...it's about tiiiiiiiiiiiiiime you noticed!"

She took a theatrical bow towards the foxes and fairies, as Hannah ran to hug her, and the whole clearing burst into applause.

CHAPTER TWELVE

The next day, we were exhausted.

Dad kept looking at us and mumbling about how too much fresh air might actually be dangerous. But after lunch, he made us go for a walk anyway.

On the way, we passed the farmhouse, where the farmer and his wife were back to normal. We could hear them arguing.

"It's an absolute pigsty in here!" yelled the Farmer. **"I'm going on the internet to learn about that woman who makes you throw everything**

away."

"Well, take a bath first!" she yelled back. **"You smell like you've been swimming in a bin."**

Dad grinned.

"Ah, the peace and quiet of the countryside," he chuckled.

The fairies had decided to work all night to clean up the forest. And, now the magic spell had been broken, the magpies were helping too.

The litter was all gone.

"Well, Mr Farmer might be a bit odd, but he

does keep things really clean," said Dad, as we walked along by the river.

Hannah and I shared a secret smile.

"Oh dear!" said Mum. "He's missed one."

Down on the bank was a single crisp packet.

"I'm taking it out!" said Hannah, crossly.

"No. I'll get it," said Mum. "Litter can be very dangerous."

"You are so right, Mum!" agreed Hannah, giving me a wink.

"Mum?" I asked. "When we get home, can we do something about litter?"

Mum thought.

"What about a litter pick?" she said. "We could get some proper equipment; gloves and pickers and things!"

"That would be great," I said.

"Thanks, Mum!" said Hannah, hugging her.

"Hey, look!" said Dad, pointing into the water. "Little baby frogs. They're called **froggles,** you know!"

Above us in the trees, I could hear Sugar

giggling. The toys had been helping with the clean-up operation. One of the fox fairies had healed Sugar's wing so she was as good as new.

"Baby frogs are called tadpoles, Dad!" I said.

Dad scratched his head.

"Actually, they could be baby **toads,**" he said, ignoring me, "and of course *they* are called **toad-poles.**"

"That's rubbish," said Mum, laughing.

"Rubbish!" agreed a squeaky voice.

Mum frowned, looking around the forest.

"**Weird** echoes in these woods," said Mum, finally.

"Ah, that'll be to do with the fairies," said Dad, nodding wisely.

"Come on," said Mum, rolling her eyes. "Let's go and start the barbecue."

"Can it be a **two marshmallow** night?" asked Dad, hopefully.

Mum grinned.

"Well, we **are** on holiday," she said. **"Why not!"**

Quiz: Which fairy are you?

1. Your teacher asks you a question you can't answer. Do you:

a) Say "I don't know. Sorry."

b) That would never happen. This question is ridiculous.

c) Hold out your throwing knives and ask "Three ways to die- which do you choose?"

2. You are woken by an ant, stepping loudly by your ear. Do you:

a) Go back to sleep.

b) Design a perfect ant-silencing solution.

c) Chase the ant with your flaming sword, screaming "BE QUIET YOU FOOL, YOU'LL WAKE EVERYONE UP!"

3. Father Christmas brings you a red and green candy cane when you specifically asked for a green and red one. Do you:

a) Enjoy the delicious candy cane.

b) Scientifically analyse the difference between green and red, and red and green.

c) Chase him across the rooftops, hurling ninja stars and screaming "DIE! YOU CANDY-MIXING FOOL!"

4. The postman leaves your letter box open after delivering the mail. Do you:

a) Close it. It was probably an innocent mistake.

b) Design the perfect self-closing letterbox so it doesn't happen again.

c) Chase the postman down the street with a battle axe, screaming "CLOSE IT NEXT TIME YOU DRAUGHT-CREATING FOOL!"

If you answered mostly A, you're a fox fairy. Mostly B, you're an owl fairy. Mostly C, you're a mole fairy. And possibly a bit crazy. Maybe have a nice calming cup of tea and a lie down somewhere.

Can you make up a song for Sugar?

Draw yourself riding Blaze!

For more fun activities visit www.jennyyork.com

Audiobooks

SUGAR + BLAZE
THAT'S
RUBBISH!

Jenny York

SUGAR + BLAZE
PRINCE CHARM-BIN!

Jenny York

SUGAR + BL
TINSELPANTS!

Jenny York

AR + BLAZE
NUTS!

Jenny York

Coming Soon!

Printed in Poland
by Amazon Fulfillment
Poland Sp. z o.o., Wrocław

89956638R00068